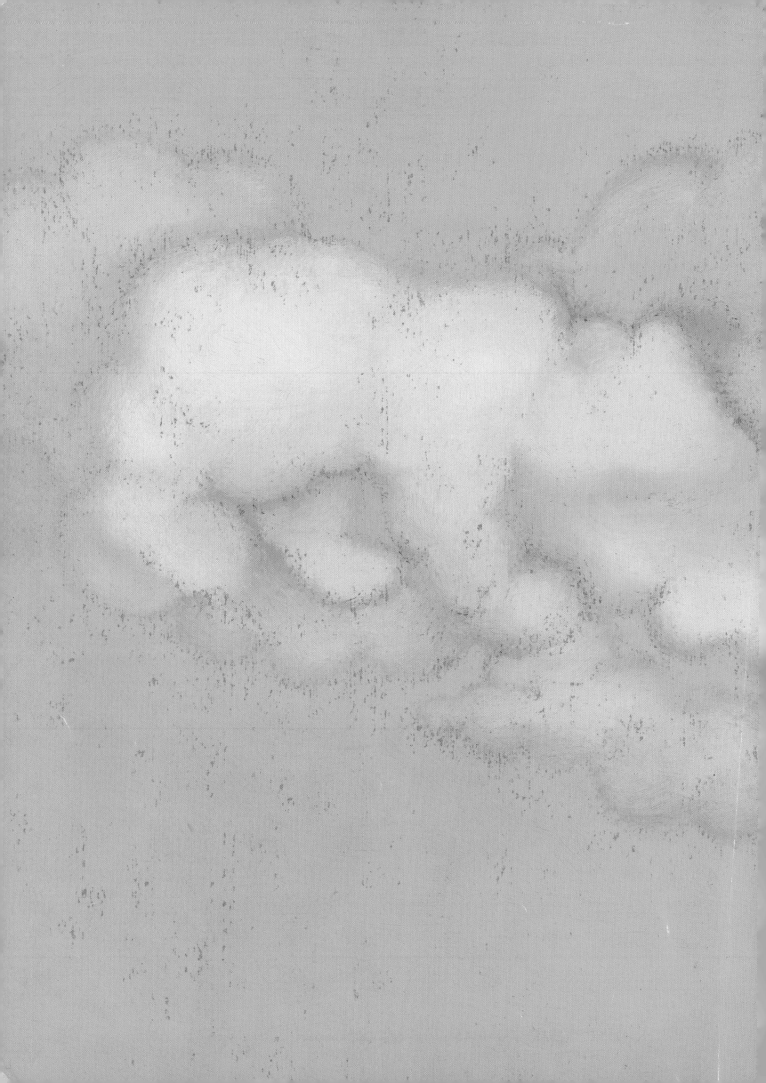

First published in the United States, Great Britain, Canada,
Australia, and New Zealand in 2003 by North-South Books,
an imprint of Nord-Süd Verlag AG, Gossau Zürich, Switzerland.

Distributed in the United States by North-South Books Inc., New York.

Library of Congress Cataloging-in-Publication Data is available.
A CIP catalogue record for this book is available from The British Library.
ISBN 0-7358-1799-5 (trade edition)
1 3 5 7 9 HC 10 8 6 4 2
ISBN 0-7358-1800-2 (library edition)
1 3 5 7 9 LE 10 8 6 4 2

Printed in Belgium

For more information about our books, and the authors and artists
who create them, visit our web site: www.northsouth.com

Bear's Last Journey

BY Udo Weigelt
ILLUSTRATED BY Cristina Kadmon

Translated by Sibylle Kazeroid

North-South Books
New York / London

"Bear is sick!" cried Hare as he ran through the forest.
"Bear is sick!"

When the animals heard this news, they all hurried to Bear's den.

"Shhh," said Badger as they approached the den. "Bear
needs to rest."

The animals were quiet. They all liked the bear very much.

And he was already very old. No animal could remember
a time when the bear hadn't been around.

"Why is it so quiet out there?" Bear suddenly called. "This is terrible! Where is everybody?"

With that all the animals went into his den. But they were quiet about it.

Bear really did look ill. Some of the animals were even a little frightened by how changed he was.

"What's the matter?" asked the little fox, anxiously pricking up his ears.